D1146388

954 - S640
954 - 0767

Enid Blyton's
TELL-A-STORY BOOK

The Little Sugar House and other stories

This book belongs to Alexandra Danielle Mazal Reed. If it is lost please return it to her or else, her brother will be out to get you and when he finds you he will nail you to a tree and throw darts at you.

sing Signed (her brother).

The Bear and the Duck

ONCE upon a time there were two toys, a bear and a duck. They lived on the top shelf in the toy-shop, and they had been there for a whole year. Fancy that! A whole year!

They were very unhappy about it. It was dreadful not to be sold. They got dustier and dustier, and at last they almost gave up hope of ever having a little boy or girl to own them.

You see, by some mistake, the duck had a bear's growl and the bear had a duck's quack. It was most upsetting. Whenever the bear was squeezed in his middle, he said "QUACK!" very loudly indeed—- and whenever the duck was squeezed she said "GRRR-RRRRRR!"

The shop-keeper had tried to sell them, but she couldn't, and that was why she had put them away on the top shelf.

One day a little girl came into the shop with her mother. She was seven years old that day, and she had come to spend the money that her granny had given her for her birthday.

"I want a duck and a bear," she said. Then she pointed up to the shelf. "Oh, look!" she said. "There are two there, just the size I want."

The shop-keeper took them down from the top shelf—and oh, how excited the duck and bear felt when they thought they really might be sold to this nice little girl!

"Do they say anything?" she asked.

"Well," said the shop-keeper, "it's rather funny. The bear quacks like a duck, and the duck growls like a bear. A mistake was made, and it is impossible to put it right."

The little girl pressed the bear and he had to quack loudly. Then she pressed the duck and it had to growl—grrr-rrrrrr!

"Oh dear," said the little girl, disappointed, "what a pity! I don't like a bear to quack and a duck to growl. It's all wrong. I'm afraid I don't want them."

The bear and the duck could have cried. The little girl looked at them again, and they looked so sad that she felt sorry for them.

"I'll see if I can get a bear that growls properly and a duck that quacks in the right way somewhere else," she said. "But if I can't—well, I might come back and buy these two."

"Very well," said the shop-keeper, and she put the two toys back on the top shelf again. They watched the little girl take her mother's hand and go out of the shop. They felt most unhappy. To think they could have been sold and gone to the same nursery to live with a nice little girl like that!

That night the bear spoke to the duck. "Quack!" he said. "Duck, listen to me. It's quite time we did something to help ourselves."

"Grrr-rrrrrr!" said the duck. "I agree with you. But what can we do?"

"Quack," said the bear thinking hard. "We will go to the Little Wise Woman on the Hill, and ask for her help. Maybe she can do something for us."

"Grrr-rrrrrr, goodness me!" said the duck in surprise. "Dare we?"

"Quack! Certainly!" said the bear, and he jumped down from the shelf. The duck followed and they went to the window, which was open at the bottom. Out they went, and walked over the wet grass. The duck had to waddle rather than walk, so they couldn't go very fast.

At last they came to the hill where the Little Wise Woman lived. Her cottage was at the top and the two toys could see that it was lighted up gaily.

"Perhaps she has a party tonight," said the duck, out of breath; "I do hope she hasn't."

But she had—and just as the two toys got to the cottage the guests began to go. Out went Dame Big-Feet, the witch, on her broom-stick, and with her flew her black cat. Out went Mrs. Twinkle, the fat woman who sold balloons all day and made spells all night. After her went Mister Poker-Man, who was as tall and as thin as a poker, and last of all

JOYCE JANTALO

went little Roll-Around, who was as round as a ball, and rolled down the hill instead of walking.

"They have nearly gone," whispered the duck to the bear. "Let's wait outside till the cottage is empty."

So they waited in a corner until all the good-byes were said, and then they crept out. They peeped in at the window, and to their great surprise they saw the Little Wise Woman sitting on a chair, groaning and crying.

"Oh my, oh my!" she said. "I've got such a headache, and there's all this mess to clear up before I go to bed."

The bear and the duck couldn't bear to see her so unhappy. They went in at the door, and spoke to the Little Wise Woman.

"We will clear up everything for you," said the bear. "Don't worry. The duck will help you to get to bed, and will make you a nice cup of tea, and give you a hot-water bottle; and I will sweep up all the mess and clear the table and wash up."

The Little Wise Woman was so surprised that she didn't know what to say.

"Why, you're from the toy-shop," she said at last. "However did you manage to get here tonight?"

"Never mind," said the bear, determined not to talk about his own troubles now. "You just get to bed, Little Wise Woman, and go to sleep. We'll do everything else."

"Grrr-rrrrrr!" growled the duck kindly much to

the Little Wise Woman's surprise.

"Quack!" said the bear, and surprised her still more. Then she remembered that her friend, the toy-shop woman, had told her about a bear who quacked and a duck who growled, and she thought these must be the two queer toys. How kind they were to come and look after her like this, just when she felt ill and had so much to do!

The duck took her into the bedroom and helped her to undress. She made a cup of nice hot tea, and

gave her a hot-water bottle. Then she tucked her into bed, turned out the light, and left her to go to sleep. The duck was not going to worry the Little Wise Woman about her own troubles now. Not she!

The bear was very busy, too. He cleared all the dirty dishes off the table, and washed them up. He put them neatly away, and swept the floor. Then he put the cakes into their tins and the biscuits into their jars, and put the lids on. He was very hungry, but of course he didn't dream of taking even half a biscuit. He knew it would be wrong, and he was a very good little bear.

Just as he had finished his work the duck came creeping out of the bedroom.

"She's almost asleep!" she said in a whisper. "We'd better go."

"I'm not quite asleep," said the Little Wise Woman in a drowsy voice. "Before you go, look in my kitchen drawer. You will find two boxes of pills there. Bear, take a yellow pill. Duck, take a blue one. You won't be sorry you came to help me tonight."

"Thank you," said the bear, astonished.

He knew that the Little Wise Woman had many marvellous spells, and he wondered what would happen when he and the duck swallowed the pills. Perhaps he would grow beautiful whiskers, and maybe the duck would grow a wonderful tail.

He took a yellow pill, and the duck swallowed a blue one. Then they carefully shut the kitchen drawer, called good-night to the Little Wise Woman and went out into the night.

They were very tired when they got back to the toy-shop. They climbed up to their shelf, leaned back against the wall, and fell fast asleep at once.

They didn't wake up till the sun was shining into the shop. The door-bell woke them with a jump and they sat up. They saw the same little girl who had come to the shop the day before. She looked up at their shelf and pointed to them.

"May I see that duck and bear again?" she asked. "I couldn't find any just their size yesterday, so I've come back to see them again."

The shop-keeper lifted them down. The little girl looked at them.

"It *is* a pity the duck growls and the bear quacks," she said. "They are such nice toys."

She pressed the duck in the middle—and to everyone's enormous surprise the duck said "QUACK" very loudly indeed. The most surprised of all was the duck herself. She had never in her life before said Quack, and it felt very funny.

Then the little girl squeezed the bear, and to his joy and astonishment he growled!

"GRRR-RRRRRR!" he went. Just like that!

"What a funny thing," said the little girl. "Yesterday they did just the opposite. Have you had them mended?"

"No," said the shop-keeper, just as surprised as the little girl. "They've not been taken down from their shelf since you went out of the shop. I can't think what has happened."

The little girl pressed the bear and the duck again.

"Grrr-rrrrrr!" growled the bear. "Quack!" said the duck. They were both most delighted. So that was what the pills of the Little Wise Woman had done—made their voices perfectly all right. How lovely!

"Well, I will buy them now," said the little girl. "There's nothing wrong with them at all, and they are just what I wanted. I think the bear is lovely and the duck is a dear. I shall love them very much."

How pleased the two toys were when they heard that! They meant to love the little girl too, and when the shop-keeper popped them into a box, put some paper round it and tied it with string, they hugged one another hard.

They hugged each other so hard that the duck had to say "Quack!" and the bear had to say "Grrr-rrrrrr!"

"Listen to that!" said the little girl, laughing. "They're saying that they are glad to come home with me."

The duck lives in the little girl's toy-cupboard now, and the bear lives in the doll's pram with Angelina the doll. They are very happy indeed, and you should just hear the duck say "Quack!" and the bear say "Grrr-rrrrrr!" whenever the little girl plays with them. They have quite the loudest voices in the nursery.

A Fairy Secret

THIS is an old story which maybe you have heard before—but the secret is such a good one that I am sure you would like to hear it again!

The fairy-folk have very few things to call their own, especially the fairies that live in the flowers. Some of them have an extra shawl to wear on cold nights and some have an extra necklace for a party. But all of them have special dancing-sandals, little goldy ones that shine as they dance at night.

Now the field-mice, whose feet are as tiny as the fairies' own feet, liked to find these goldy sandals and wear them! Then they, too, could dance lightly for hours. So wherever the fairy-folk hid their sandals, the mice hunted for them and stole them!

"It's too bad," said the fairies one night when they went to fetch their dancing-shoes from under the violet leaves where they had hidden them. "Our shoes are all gone again!"

"It's those mice!" said the pixies angrily.

"We shan't be able to dance for weeks now,"

sighed the elves. "We haven't any money at all to go and buy new sandals from the cobbler."

After a while the little folk had some more shoes made, and very pleased they were with them too, for the cobbler had put tiny buckles on each pair of sandals, with a winking dewdrop for a glittering stone in the middle!

"Those shoes are too precious to be stolen by those naughty little mice!" said the elves, as they tried them on.

"We will hide them at the bottom of a worm-hole," said the pixies. So, after the dance that night, that is what they did. They tied their shoes together in a long string and pushed them down to the bottom of an empty worm-hole.

But a bright-eyed mouse had seen them and his whiskers twitched with delight. "More shoes! Ha, mouse-feet will go tapping over the fields tomorrow, dancing the Mouse-Walk and the Tail-Parade! I'll go and tell the others."

He ran off. The mice were soon round the hole in the early morning sun, when the fairies were sleeping soundly in the buttercups and other flowers, tired after their night's play.

The mice put down their little front paws and tried to pull up the dancing-sandals. But they couldn't reach far enough down the hole.

"I'll make a burrow from my hole to the worm-hole!" said the first mouse, and he scampered down his hole near by. He soon made a passage to the worm-hole, dragged out the shoes into his own burrow and divided them among the small-footed mice. How grand they looked in their tip-tapping golden sandals!

But the fairies were very sad when they found that their new shoes had been stolen. They hunted for them everywhere, but the mice had hidden them well and they never found them again.

"It's no use our buying new shoes and having them stolen each time like this," said the pixies.

"Then we must find some really good hiding-place!" said the fairies. "And we will put a spell on our shoes now, so that if anyone drags them from their hiding-place they will no longer be shoes!"

So they hunted and hunted to find a good place.

"The bottom of the poppies would be good," said a pixie. "We could cover the shoes with the black stamens."

"That would make them so black, though," said an elf. "No, that won't do. What about inside a foxglove bell?"

"Silly idea!" said the fairies at once. "The bumble-bees go there every day, and they would buzz the news all round at once if they found our shoes tucked away near the nectar at the back. Think again, elf."

So the elf thought again—and this time she thought of a really good hiding-place, where she was sure the mice would never look. So all the little folk hid their shoes there after the next dance—and they put a spell on them too, so that the sandals would change into something else if anyone took them!

The mice hunted everywhere. They sniffed inside the buttercups, they blacked their noses by looking in the sooty middle of the poppies, they hunted in every worm-hole they could find, making the worms very angry indeed.

But they couldn't find them! Not one sandal could they see, and they haven't discovered the fairies' secret yet!

Would you like to know it? Well I'll tell you—but don't try to take the sandals, will you, for they certainly won't *be* fairy dancing-shoes any longer if you pull them away from their hiding-place!

If you want to see them, go and hunt for the big white dead-nettle flowers that grow everywhere by the fields and hedges and waysides. Look inside the flowers, but look in the *top* of the flower, not the bottom—and there, neatly arranged in their pairs, you will see the hidden goldy sandals of the little folk!

Isn't it a good hiding-place? Touch the little shoes gently, and maybe they will leave magic on your finger that will bring you good luck all that day!

Pip and the Badger

"PIP!" called Aunt Twinkle, "it's Saturday and I'm busy. Will you go and do my shopping for me?"

"Yes, Aunt," said Pip; "but I hope I don't have to stand in many queues. It's so cold!"

"Well, put on your new scarf and your woolly coat," said Aunt Twinkle. "Here's the basket and shopping list. Now, off you go!"

Pip went off rather gloomily. He thought he would go through the wood because he might meet one of his friends, Sandy the rabbit, there.

But he didn't meet Sandy. He met somebody else! He was passing an ivy-covered bank when he heard a queer snorting noise. Whatever could it be?

Some leaves and sand came flying from the bank—and then Pip saw a striped, black-and-white head peeping out of a hole. It was a big head, and it made Pip jump with fright. He turned to run away.

"Wait, wait!" called a voice. "What are you frightened of, silly? I'm only Brock the badger."

"Oh," said Pip, stopping. "Of course—you've

been asleep all the winter, haven't you? Are you going to wake up now and come out and play?"

"I don't know," said the badger. "I want to know what date it is, first."

"Well, it's Saturday, February the first," said Pip. "But why do you want to know the date?"

"For a very good reason!" said the badger. "Didn't you know that on the *second* of February I poke my nose out of my den to see what the weather's like? If it is warm and the grass is green I go back to sleep again, because I know there is still bitter weather to come. But if the snow is on the ground and the frost is about, I wake up properly and come out, I know that the winter is over, you see. Don't you know the old rhyme:

> "If Candlemas Day be fair and bright,
>   Winter will have another flight;
>   But if Candlemas Day be clouds and rain
>   Winter has gone and will not come again."

"Well, that seems queer to me," said Pip. "You're a day early, Brock. It's tomorrow you have to poke your nose out. Go back! I just hope that the snow is on the ground when you look out tomorrow; then we'll know that the spring will soon be here!"

The badger went back into his den. He will be poking his nose out tomorrow to see what the weather is like. Let's hope that snow is on the ground, then spring will be just round the corner! Wise old fellow, the badger, isn't he?

A Surprise
for the Wagtails

A PAIR of wagtails built their nest in some creeper that straggled over a roof. It was a nice nest, and soon it had four little eggs in it.

"Now, I must sit on them to keep them warm," said the hen wagtail. But first she flew off with her mate to catch some of the midges flying in the sunshine.

Whilst she was gone a big cuckoo saw the nest. Now, the cuckoo had made no nest, but she had to have one to put her egg in. So, whilst the wagtails were away, the cuckoo put her egg into their nest, and took out one of the eggs already there. Then she flew off, cuckooing loudly.

The wagtails came back. They didn't notice that one of the eggs was a little larger and not quite the same colour as the others. The hen wagtail sat down to keep them warm. She felt very happy. It is always nice for a bird to feel her warm little eggs under her.

Two of the eggs hatched out. One little bird was bigger than the other. He was very bare and black and ugly. He couldn't bear to feel the two eggs near him, nor could he bear to feel the other baby bird pressing against him. When the wagtails had left the nest for a little while, he managed to get one of the eggs on to his back, climbed up to the edge of the nest with it, and tipped it over! Out it went and smashed on the roof.

Then he sank down into the nest, tired out. But it wasn't long before he got the other egg on to his back and tipped that out too!

Then it was the turn of the baby bird. After a lot of struggling the tiny cuckoo got the baby wagtail on to his back, climbed slowly up to the edge of the nest, and tipped him out as well. He squeaked feebly, but no bird seemed to notice him.

Now the baby cuckoo was happy. He had the nest to himself. He settled down and waited for food.

The wagtails were surprised when they found that only one bird was in the nest. "But see how big he is!" they cried. "He seems to grow almost as we look at him. What a fine bird he will be! Finer and bigger than any other wagtail in the garden."

They fed him well. They were very proud of him. They called the other birds to see him. "Did you ever know a finer wagtail baby?" they said. "Isn't he magnificent?"

Soon the baby filled the nest. Then he was too big for it. He had to stand outside on the roof. He called piercingly all day long, because he was hungry, and soon other birds began to feed him too. Always his big beak seemed to be open!

Then the wagtails had to stand on his shoulder to feed him, for he grew far bigger than they were. How proud they were of him. They talked to the other birds about him, and boasted each day of the marvellous child.

They took him about with them to teach him to feed himself—and one day, what a shock they got! He opened his beak and made a most peculiar noise.

"He's trying to sing!" said the wagtails. "He's trying to say 'chissic, chissic', as we do!"

But he wasn't. He was trying to call his first loud "cuckoo!" And when he did, what a shock for the poor wagtails!

"Oh, he's a cuckoo, he's a cuckoo!" they cried.

The other birds laughed. "We thought he was," they said. "You were a pair of cuckoos, too, to think he was a wagtail!"

Treacle-Pudding Town

THOMAS loved treacle pudding. His mother would often make a great big one for her four children, with golden syrup poured all over it. Thomas thought it was the nicest pudding in the world.

He was greedy. He ate up his slice of pudding as quickly as he could, so that he could have a second helping before anyone else did.

"Don't gobble, Thomas," his mother said. But as he gobbled because he wanted to have more than anybody else, he just went on gobbling.

He gobbled his bread-and-butter at tea-time so that he could have more cakes than anybody, especially if there was a chocolate cake. The other children were cross with him. "It isn't fair," they said. "You are greedy, Thomas, and you always try to have more than your fair share!"

One day there was a fine treacle pudding for dinner. Thomas had two big helpings—and then his mother said the rest of the pudding was to be saved for Ellen his sister, who was going to be late for dinner that day. Thomas watched his mother put it into the larder. He longed and longed for just another piece, although he had really had quite enough.

His mother went out into the garden to put some clothes on the line. Thomas opened the larder door and peeped inside. There was the rest of the treacle pudding, still on the dish, warm and sticky! Thomas looked and looked at it.

And then, what do you think he did? He stole up to the shelf, took a spoon and gobbled up the rest of that pudding!

Wasn't he horrid? When he had finished it all, he was frightened. What would his mother say? What would his sister do? She would smack him hard and pull his hair, because when she flew into a temper she was very rough.

Thomas ran down the garden, squeezed through the hedge at the bottom, and sat in the field there.

"I do wish I needn't go home again," he said to himself. "I *shall* get into trouble when I do!"

He sighed a heavy sigh, and a small man hurrying by stopped and looked at him in surprise.

"What's the matter?" he asked.

"Oh, I just don't want to go back home," said Thomas. "I'm afraid I shall be smacked if I do."

"Poor boy!" said the little man. He had a long beard reaching nearly to his toes, and the brightest green eyes that Thomas had ever seen. "Well, why go home? Isn't there somewhere else you can go?"

"No," said Thomas. "But oh, how I wish I could go to some place where I could have treacle pudding and chocolate cake, as much as ever I liked! I never have enough at home."

"Dear, dear!" said the little man. He was a brownie, though Thomas didn't know this. "Well, I think I can help you. What about coming with me to Treacle-Pudding Town? It's not very far."

Thomas could hardly believe his ears. Treacle-Pudding Town! What a wonderful place it sounded. He jumped up at once.

"I'll go," he said. "Is there really plenty of treacle pudding there?"

"Oh yes," said the brownie. "And chocolate cake too. It's a famous place for that, you know. They do nothing there but make and sell treacle puddings and chocolate cake. My cousin lives there. I'll take you to stay with him if you like. He'll be pleased to have you."

Well, greedy little Thomas was only too pleased to go. He forgot that his mother would worry about him. He forgot that he was supposed to go to school that afternoon. He just wanted to get to those puddings and cakes. So off he went with the brownie.

He went across the field, over the stile, and into the wood. And in the very middle of the wood was Treacle-Pudding Town! Thomas stood and stared at it. It was a most extraordinary place.

"Why, the houses are the shape of treacle puddings and chocolate cakes!" he said. "How funny! And look at that stream—I'm sure it's full of

treacle instead of water!"

"Here is my cousin's house," said the brownie, going into a tiny house shaped like a birthday cake. The chimneys looked like three candles smoking!

"Tippy, Tippy, are you in?" cried the brownie. "I've brought a friend to stay with you."

"Very pleased to have him, I'm sure," said Tippy, who was a little man very like his cousin. He smelt of chocolate. In fact, the whole village smelt of chocolate and treacle. Thomas liked it.

"Well, good-bye, Thomas," said the first brownie. "I hope you'll have a good time. You can eat as much as ever you like here, you know."

Thomas was so excited. "Can I really?" he said. "I didn't have much dinner. Can I have some treacle pudding?"

"Certainly," said Tippy. He went to the kitchen and came back with a white dish in which was a steaming hot pudding with yellow treacle poured all over it. "Help yourself. I don't want any."

Well, you may not believe it, but Thomas ate all that treacle pudding! Tippy saw the empty dish and grinned.

"I've another pudding in the kitchen," he said. "Will you have it?"

But, dear me, Thomas felt as if he couldn't eat even a small slice. He shook his head. "I feel as if I want to go to sleep," he said.

"I should think so," said Tippy. He showed Thomas a couch and the little boy lay down on it.

He slept till tea-time. Then he woke up. He smelt chocolate cakes baking and was glad.

"Hallo!" said Tippy, coming in to lay the tea-table. "Tea-time! New cakes!"

Thomas got up and sat at the table. Tippy put three plates on the table—one had small chocolate buns on it, one had a round chocolate cake, and one had a square one.

"Ha! No bread-and-butter!" said Thomas, pleased.

"Oh no," said Tippy. "Just cakes. Help yourself. I don't want any."

Thomas thought it was funny not to want any. Anyway, that left all the more for him! He ate all the little buns. He ate half the round chocolate cake and then he began on the square one. But, oh dear, what a pity! Before he was half-way through it, he suddenly felt as if he didn't want any more! What a waste of cake! He drank his tea and went out into the street.

All the shops sold treacle puddings and chocolate cakes—nothing else at all! Thomas looked into two or three windows and then he got rather bored with seeing the same things, and wished he could find a toy-shop. But there wasn't one.

He found some brownie children and played with them for a long time. They liked him, and asked him to go back to their home to have supper with them.

Thomas was feeling hungry again. It was a long time since tea-time. He went to their house, wondering what there would be for supper.

What do you suppose it was? Yes—a great big treacle pudding! Thomas stared at it. He wasn't so pleased to see it as he had been to see the one at dinner-time. But all the same, he managed to eat two helpings of it. Then we went back to Tippy's house and undressed to go to bed.

In the morning he was very hungry again. He wondered if there would be bacon or kippers or eggs for breakfast, and perhaps porridge, and toast and marmalade. Lovely! He ran downstairs.

But, good gracious, Tippy brought in a treacle pudding for breakfast! Thomas was really disappointed.

"You don't look pleased to see my beautiful pudding," said Tippy, offended. "Well, there's nothing else. I haven't baked any chocolate cakes yet. Eat up your pudding."

So Thomas ate it up, but somehow he didn't enjoy it. He was getting very tired of treacle pudding. And he was even more tired of it when dinner-time came and he found that there was nothing but chocolate buns and treacle pudding again. He felt as if he really *couldn't* eat any!

"If only it was rice pudding or stewed apples!" said Thomas to Tippy.

Tippy looked as cross as could be. "You horrid, ungrateful boy!" he said. "What did you want to come to Treacle-Pudding Town for? My cousin said you were a very greedy boy, and would love to eat

as much as I could cook for you—and now, the very
first dinner-time you are here, you turn up your
nose at my nice pudding. Eat it up at once, I tell
you!"

"I can't!" said poor Thomas. "I should be ill if I
did. Somehow it looks horrid to me now, that
treacle pudding!"

Tippy was very angry. He picked up the treacle
pudding and threw it straight at Thomas. It hit him
on the nose and the treacle ran down his face. Then
Tippy snowballed him with the chocolate buns.
Thomas ran out of the house, crying. He was very
unhappy and wanted his mother.

He ran through the town. He ran through the

wood. He climbed over the stile and ran across the field back to his home. He rushed up the garden and into the kitchen. There was his mother, baking chocolate cakes.

"Mother! Mother!" cried Thomas, hugging her. "Did you wonder where I had been all this time?"

"No, Thomas," said his mother in surprise. "It is only an hour since dinner."

Then Thomas knew that a day in Treacle-Pudding Town was only an hour in our world, and he was glad. But there was something he had to tell his mother.

"Mother," he said, "please forgive me—but I ate the rest of the treacle pudding out of the larder."

"Oh, Thomas, how naughty of you!" said his mother, shocked. "It's a good thing that Ellen has stayed to dinner at school, after all. You must never do such a thing again—but I will forgive you, because you have told me. Thomas, don't be a greedy little boy—no one likes greedy children."

"I won't be any more," promised Thomas.

"I expect you will be, though, at tea-time, when you see new chocolate buns on the table!" said his mother.

But she got a surprise, for Thomas wouldn't eat a single chocolate bun! And he won't eat treacle pudding either! He can't bear to see one on the table. His mother doesn't know why, so she can't understand it—but I know why Thomas has changed, don't you?

Old Mother Wrinkle

OLD Mother Wrinkle was a strange old dame. She lived in an oak tree, which had a small door so closely fitted into its trunk that nobody but Dame Wrinkle could open it. It was opened many times a day by the old dame, for always there seemed to be somebody knocking at her door.

The little folk came to ask her to take away their wrinkles. Fairies never get old as we do—but sometimes, if they are worried about anything, they frown or sulk, and then lines and wrinkles grow in their faces. Frown at yourself in the glass and see the ugly wrinkle you get!

Mother Wrinkle could always take away any wrinkle, no matter how deep it was. She would take a fairy into her round tree-room, sit her down in a chair and look at her closely.

"Ho!" she might say, "you've been feeling cross this week. There's a very nasty wrinkle right in the middle of your forehead. Sit still, please!"

Then she would rub a curious-smelling ointment on the fairy's forehead to loosen the wrinkle. Then she took up a very fine knife and carefully scraped the wrinkle off. She powdered the fairy's forehead and told her to go.

"But don't you frown any more," she would call after her. "It's a pity to spoil your pretty face."

Now Mother Wrinkle had taken wrinkles away for two hundred years, and the inside of her home was getting quite crowded with the wrinkles. She didn't like to throw them away, for she was a careful old dame. She packed them into boxes and piled them one on top of another.

But soon the boxes reached the top of her room—really, there must be a million wrinkles packed into them. What in the world could Mother Wrinkle do with them?

Now the fairies did not pay her for taking away their wrinkles. Sometimes they brought her a little pot of honey, sometimes a new shawl made of dandelion fluff—but the old dame hardly ever had any money, and she needed some badly.

"I want a new table," she said, looking at her old worn one. "I would love a rocking-chair to rock myself in when I am tired. And how I would like a pair of soft slippers for my old feet."

She told the sandy rabbit about it one day when he came to bid her good morning. He nodded his long-eared head. "Yes," he said, "you do want some new things, Mother Wrinkle. Well, why don't you sell those boxes of wrinkles and get a little money?"

"Sell the wrinkles?" cried the old dame. "Why, I'd love to—but who would buy them? Nobody! If people want to get rid of wrinkles they certainly wouldn't pay money to buy some. That's a silly idea, Sandy Rabbit!"

The rabbit lolloped off, thinking hard. He liked the old woman. She was always generous and kind. He wished he could help her. He talked to the pixies about it. He spoke to the frogs. He told the hedgehog. He spoke to the bluebell fairy—and last of all he met the little primrose fairy, and told her.

She listened carefully, and then she thought hard.

She had been very worried for the last fifty years because the primroses, which were her special care, had been dreadfully spoilt each spring by the rain. Whenever it rained the wet clung to the leaves, ran down to the centre of the plant and spoilt the pretty yellow flowers. It was such a nuisance. She had been so worried about it that Mother Wrinkle had had to scrape away about twenty wrinkles from her pretty forehead.

But now she had an idea. Suppose she took the wrinkles that the old dame had got in her boxes! Suppose she pressed them into the primrose leaves! Suppose she made them *so* wrinkled that when the rain came the wrinkles acted like little river-beds and drained the water off at once, so that it didn't soak the leaves and spoil the flowers!

"What a good idea that would be!" thought the primrose fairy joyfully. "I'll try it."

So she went to Mother Wrinkle and bought one box of wrinkles. She took them to her primrose dell and set to work. The primrose leaves, in those days, were as smooth and as thin as beech leaves—but when the fairy began to press the wrinkles into the leaves, what a difference it made!

One by one the leaves looked rough and wrinkled. In the middle of her work the rain came down, and to the fairy's delight the wrinkles acted just as she had hoped—the rain ran into them and trickled to the ground in tiny rivulets!

"Good!" said the fairy in delight. "Now listen,

primrose plants! You must grow your leaves in a rosette and point them all outwards and downwards. Then, when the rain comes, your wrinkles will let it all run away on the outside—and your flowers will be kept dry and unspoilt."

Little by little the fairy gave wrinkles to every primrose plant, and they grew well, till the woods were yellow with the flowers in spring. Mother Wrinkle was delighted to sell the old wrinkles. She bought herself a new table, a fine rocking-chair, and two pairs of soft slippers.

And now you must do something to find out if this strange little story is true. Hunt for the primrose plant—and look at the leaves. You will see the wrinkles there as sure as can be—delicate and fine—but quite enough to let the rain run away without spoiling the pale and lovely flowers.

The Thrush and His Anvil

IT was a lovely spring morning; the birds were singing, and the sun shone into Jane's room so brightly that she woke up early and jumped out of bed without waiting for Mother to come and call her.

"I must go out and see how my plants are getting on," she thought. "We have had so many wet days lately that I have not been out in the garden for quite a long time. I'll go before breakfast, while it is fine."

She dressed quickly and ran out into the garden. The air smelt warm and moist after the rain. Jane had a little piece of garden of her own which she looked after with special care, and she hoped to find that her plants had grown quite big.

So they had, but, oh dear! nearly every leaf had a piece bitten off it! Jane was most upset. She ran round the rest of the garden, and found that Daddy's plants were just the same. Lots of his young lettuces were eaten too.

She rushed back to the house and burst into the dining-room where Mummy, Daddy, and Peter were sitting down to breakfast.

"Daddy," she cried, "it's too bad; something is eating all our young plants! Something big too—not just a caterpillar or a grub."

"It's probably the snails," said Daddy. "After all, they have about fourteen thousand teeth on their tongues you know. They can do a lot of damage in one night! And there are generally a lot of them about after rain."

"Gracious—have snails got teeth on their tongues?" said Peter. "I never knew that. Fourteen thousand teeth—why, their tongues must be like rasps, then!"

"They are," said Daddy, "like files. Of course, they are not the kind of teeth you and I have, Peter! But they are very strong, and a snail can eat most of a young plant in a night, using his ribbon-tongue."

"But doesn't he wear it out?" asked Jane.

"Yes; but it is always growing," said Daddy.

"Well, what are we to do about our snails?" asked Jane. "We can't let them eat everything in the garden. There must be dozens of them about."

"Finish your breakfast," said Daddy, "and then we will go and look at the damage."

They were soon out in the garden and looking at the plants.

Suddenly Daddy stopped and pointed to something.

"Hallo!" he said. "We needn't worry much about your plague of snails. Somebody else knows about them and is dealing with them. See that stone? That

42

is the thrush's anvil—the place he comes to when he has caught a snail and wants to smash its shell."

The children saw a flint beside the path. Round it were scattered many fragments of broken shell.

"Did the thrush really have the sense to come and use this stone for an anvil?" said Peter, half doubtful.

"Well, come into the summer-house here and we'll watch," said Daddy. "It's always better to see a thing for yourself than to hear about it second-hand. Come on."

They sat down in the summer-house and waited. They didn't have to wait long. Soon a thrush with a freckled breast flew down to the stone.

"He's got a snail in his beak!" whispered Jane.

So he had. Then he began to deal with the snail. He struck it hard on the stone anvil again and again. Tap, tap, tap, tap! Tap, tap, tap tap!

"I've often heard that noise before and I didn't know what it was!" whispered Peter. "Now I shall know it's a thrush using his anvil!"

The thrush worked hard. The snail-shell was strong and it wouldn't break. The thrush beat it down with all his might. Crack!

"It's broken!" said Jane. "Now he can get at the soft body inside. He's eating the snail, Daddy."

"Poor snail!" said Peter. "But he shouldn't eat our lettuces!"

"Clever thrush!" said Daddy, getting up. "Well—I think you can leave him to deal with your snails, don't you?"

Chinky Takes a Parcel

CHINKY was doing his shopping in the pixie market. It was full today, and there were a great many people to talk to. Chinky was a chatterbox, so he loved talking.

His market-bag was full. He had no more money to spend, and it was getting near his dinner-time. "I really must go home," said Chinky, and he picked up his bag.

"Hi," called Sally Simple, "did you say you were going home? Well, just deliver this parcel to Mrs. Flip's next door to you, will you? It's for her party this afternoon."

"Certainly," said Chinky, and he took the square box, which felt very cold indeed.

"You are sure you are going straight home?" asked Sally Simple anxiously. "I don't want you to take the parcel unless you are really off home now."

"I'm going this very minute," said Chinky. "Good-bye!"

He set off home—but he hadn't gone far before he met Dame Giggle, and she had a funny story to tell him. He listened and laughed, and then he

thought of a *much* funnier story to tell Dame Giggle.

So it was quite ten minutes before he set off home again—and then who should he meet but Old Man Grumble, who stopped him and shook hands. Chinky hadn't seen Old Man Grumble for a long time, and he had a lot of news to tell him. He talked and he talked, and Old Man Grumble hadn't even time to get one grumble in!

"You *are* a chatterbox, Chinky," he said at last. "Good-bye! Perhaps you'll let me get a word in when next we meet."

Chinky set off again. The square cold parcel that he was carrying for Sally Simple seemed to have got very soft and squashy now. It was no longer cold either. It was rather warm and sticky!

"Goodness! I wonder what's in this parcel?" thought Chinky, hugging it under his arm.

A little drop of yellow juice ran out of one corner and dripped down Chinky's leg. It was ice-cream in the parcel—a big yellow brick of it, that Mrs. Flip had ordered for her party. She meant to put it into her freezing-machine when she got it, and then it would keep cold and icy till four o'clock.

Chinky went on his way humming. Some more ice-cream melted and ran down his leg. Chinky didn't know. He was nodding excitedly at little Fairy Long-wings, who was standing at her gate.

"Hallo, Long-wings!" called Chinky. "Glad to see you back. How did you enjoy your holiday?"

And, dear me, he stood talking at Long-wings' gate for ten minutes. Long-wings didn't tell him a word about her holiday, for Chinky was so busy chattering about himself and his garden and his shopping. And all the time the ice-cream dripped down his leg.

Well, when at last he arrived at Mrs. Flip's the box was almost flat and empty. He handed it to Mrs. Flip, and she looked at it in dismay.

"My ice-cream for the party!" she cried. "It's all melted! Look at your clothes, Chinky—what a mess they are in! Well, really, you might have brought it to me at once! I suppose Sally Simple gave it to you, thinking that you were coming straight home!"

"Well, so I did!" said Chinky indignantly. "I came *straight* home, as straight as could be!"

"I don't believe you," said Mrs. Flip. "I know you, Chinky—the worst chatterbox in town! Oh yes! You met Mr. So-and-so, and you talked to him for ages—and you saw Mrs. This-and-that, and you chatted for ten minutes—and you came across Dame Such-and-such, and you had a good long talk! And all the time my ice-cream was melting. Take it! I don't want it now—it's just an empty box."

She threw it at Chinky and it hit him on the nose. He was very angry. He shook his fist at Mrs. Flip and shouted, "I shan't come to your party now! I just shan't come!"

"Well, don't then!" said Mrs. Flip, and she went

inside and banged her door. Chinky banged his.

Soon there was the sound of the ringing of a tricycle bell, and along came the ice-cream man. Mrs. Flip heard him and out she ran. She bought the biggest ice-cream brick he had, all pink and yellow. She popped it into her freezing-machine for the party that afternoon.

And when Chinky looked out of his window at half-past four, he saw everyone busy eating ice-creams in Mrs. Flip's garden, as happy as could be. Wasn't he cross!

"Why didn't I go straight home as I said I would? Why did I say I wouldn't go to the party? I talk too much, that's what's the matter with me!" said poor Chinky.

But chatterboxes can't be stopped—you try stopping one, and see!

The Little Sugar House

MRS. BISCUIT kept a cake-shop in Tweedle Village. All the boys and girls liked her shop because she had such exciting things in the window —gingerbread men, pastry cats and dogs, chocolate horses, and fine iced cakes.

Mrs. Biscuit would have been a very nice woman if only she hadn't told so many stories. She really didn't seem to know *how* to tell the truth.

"Was this cake baked today?" a customer would ask. "Is it quite fresh?"

"Oh yes, madam, it's just new," Mrs. Biscuit would answer, knowing quite well that the cake was stale and dry.

Mrs. Biscuit was mean, too. She never gave anything away if she could help it, not even broken bits of stale cake. She made those into puddings for herself.

Now one day she thought she would make a very fine iced cake and put it into the middle of her window to make people stare.

"If they come and look at my iced cake they will see my buns, my biscuits, and other things," thought Mrs. Biscuit, "and perhaps they will buy them."

So she made a beautiful iced cake with pink roses all round the edge. But she didn't know what to put in the middle.

"I think I'll make a little sugar house," she said to herself. "It shall have windows and a door and two chimneys. Everyone will be delighted to see it."

So she made a wonderful little house all out of sugar. She gave it two red chimneys, four windows, and a little brown door made of chocolate. She put pink sugar roses on the walls, and when it had set hard she popped it on the very top of her big cake. Then she put it into the window.

At first everyone came to look at it—but after a little while they thought it was dull.

"Why don't you put someone into your house?" asked a little girl. "Houses are meant to be lived in, aren't they, even sugar houses? Why don't you go to the Very-Little-Goblins and ask one to live in your sugar house? Then people would come every day to see him opening the chocolate door and looking out of the sugar windows at the pink roses."

Well, Mrs. Biscuit thought that was a very good idea. She put on her bonnet and went to where the Very-Little-Goblins lived in their mushroom houses.

"Would one of you like to come and live in a sugar house with pink roses on the walls?" she asked. "It's not like your mushroom houses, up one night and gone the next, so that you have to keep on moving. It stays on my big iced cake for weeks and weeks, and is very beautiful indeed."

The Very-Little-Goblins came out of their mushroom houses and stared at her.

"We have heard that you tell stories," said their chief goblin. "We are very truthful people, you know, and we couldn't live with anyone who didn't tell the truth."

."Of course I tell the truth!" said Mrs. Biscuit crossly. "Why, I've never told a story in my life!"

"Well, that's splendid," said the chief goblin,

quite believing her. "I shall be very pleased to let my eldest son come and live in your little sugar house tomorrow."

"Thank you," said Mrs. Biscuit, delighted, and she went home.

Soon everyone knew that one of the Very-Little-Goblins was going to live on the big iced cake in the window, and all the children of Tweedle Village were tremendously excited.

The next day Twinkle, the Very-Little-Goblin, arrived at Mrs. Biscuit's shop. She lifted him up on to the iced cake in the window and showed him the sugar house. He was simply delighted with it.

He opened the little chocolate door and went inside. He had brought no furniture with him, so he asked Mrs. Biscuit if she would make him a little chocolate bed, two sugar chairs, and a chocolate table. He said he would put up curtains at the windows and buy a little carpet for the floor.

Soon the sugar house was quite ready for him, and all the children of the village came to peep at it. It was most exciting to see the goblin open the door and shake his little mats. It was lovely to see him draw the curtains and lean out of the window. Sometimes he would carry his chocolate table and one of his sugar chairs on to the big sugary space outside the little house, and have his dinner there.

Mrs. Biscuit did such a lot of trade. A great many people came into the shop to see the iced cake with its sugar house, and of course they had to buy something, so Mrs. Biscuit began to be quite rich.

For a little while she remembered to tell the truth to people—and then she forgot.

"Is this chocolate cake fresh?" asked Dame Tippy one morning.

"Oh yes, quite!" said Mrs. Biscuit untruthfully, for the cake had been baked more than a week ago.

"Oh, you story-teller!" cried a tiny voice, and the Very-Little-Goblin peeped out of the sugar house. "You baked that last week."

"Dear, dear, so I did!" said Mrs. Biscuit crossly, very angry to hear the goblin's voice. "Take this one instead, Dame Tippy."

The next day a little girl came in for ten pence-worth of fresh buns. Mrs. Biscuit quickly took six stale ones from a tray at the back of the shop and popped them into a bag.

"These are nice and new," she said to the little girl.

"You naughty story-teller! They're as hard as bricks!" cried the little goblin, poking his head out of the window of the sugar house.

"You be quiet! These buns were only baked this morning," said Mrs. Biscuit angrily.

"Oooh, the story-teller! Oh, little girl, don't give her your ten pence. She's telling you stories!"

The little girl ran out of the shop with her ten pence in her hand, but Mrs. Biscuit called her back.

"I'm only joking with you," she said to the child. "See, here are some lovely new buns I baked early this morning."

"Yes, take those," cried the goblin. They're all right."

When the little girl had gone, Mrs. Biscuit turned to grumble at the goblin. To her surprise he was rolling up his carpet and taking down his curtains.

"What are you doing?" she asked.

"Going home," answered the goblin. "You don't suppose I'm going to stay here with a nasty old woman who tells stories, do you? We Very-Little-Goblins hate that!"

"Oh, don't go," begged Mrs. Biscuit. "Don't go! Everyone will wonder why you've gone."

"Oh no, they won't because I shall tell them," said the goblin, tying up his carpet into a roll.

"Please, please, goblin, stay with me. I'll make you a beautiful little garden-seat out of chocolate and ginger if you'll only stay," begged Mrs. Biscuit. "And I won't tell stories any more, I promise you."

"Well, if you do, I'll tell people the truth," said the goblin, unrolling his carpet again. "So you be careful, Mrs. Biscuit."

Mrs. Biscuit was very careful for a few days and the goblin didn't speak a word. Then one morning, a poor beggar-woman came in and asked Mrs. Biscuit for a stale cake.

"A stale cake? Why, I haven't such a thing in the place!" cried Mrs. Biscuit. "Be off with you!"

"Oh, you mean old woman!" cried the goblin's tiny voice, and he flung open his chocolate front door. "Where are those cakes you baked last Thursday and haven't sold yet?"

"I've eaten them myself," said Mrs. Biscuit in a rage. "Mind your own business!"

"You're a story-teller," said the goblin. "There they are up on that shelf. You give them to the poor beggar-woman this very minute, or I'll go back to Mushroom Town."

Mrs. Biscuit dragged the cakes down, put them into a bag and threw them across the counter. The beggar-woman thanked her and went off with them.

Mrs. Biscuit didn't care to say anything to the goblin, but she was very angry. He went into his sugar house and slammed the door. He was angry too, to think that anyone could be so mean.

That afternoon a thin little boy crept into the shop and asked for a stale crust. He was dreadfully hungry, and Mrs. Biscuit stared at him crossly. Another beggar!

She was just going to say that she had no stale crusts when she saw the goblin peeping at her out of one of the windows of his sugar house. She hurriedly took down half a stale loaf and gave it to the little boy.

He was so gateful that he took her plump hand and kissed it. It was the first time that Mrs. Biscuit had been kissed for years, and dear me, she *did* like it! She suddenly smiled at the little boy, and felt sorry to see how thin he was. And then she took down a fine new chocolate cake, and gave it to him.

"Oh!" he said in delight. "You kind woman! Is that really for me?"

He went out of the shop singing. Mrs. Biscuit looked at the place on her hand where the little boy had kissed it, and a nice warm feeling crept into her heart. It was really rather pleasant to be kind, she thought. She would try it again.

She looked up and saw a crowd of people looking in at her window. And she saw that the goblin was doing a strange, light-hearted little dance round and round the top of the cake, making all the passers-by stare in surprise.

"What are you doing that for?" she asked in astonishment.

"Oh, I'm so pleased to see you do a kind act that I've got to dance!" said the tiny goblin. Everyone watched him, and soon quite a dozen people came in to buy cakes. Mrs. Biscuit did a good morning's trade.

The next time someone came begging, Mrs. Biscuit decided to be kind and generous again, to get the nice warm feeling in her heart. So she packed up a cherry-pie in a box and put some ginger buns in a bag for the old man who came asking for a crust. He was so surprised and delighted that he could hardly say thank you. The little goblin threw open his door and began to sing a loud song all about Mrs. Biscuit's kindness, and soon half the village came to hear it. Mrs. Biscuit blushed red, and didn't know where to look.

Then Mr. Straw, the farmer, came to buy a big ginger cake for his wife's birthday. Now, there were two ginger cakes in the shop, one baked a good time back and one baked that very morning. Mrs. Biscuit took up the stale one and popped it into a bag.

"You're sure that's fresh, now?" said Farmer Straw. Mrs. Biscuit opened her mouth to say untruthfully that it was, when she stopped.

No, that would be a mean unkind thing to say, especially when the cake was for Mrs. Straw's birthday.

"Er—well, no, this one isn't very fresh," she said.

"I'll give you a fresher one, only baked this morning."

The little goblin, who was peeping out of his window, ready to cry out that she was a story-teller, gave a shout of delight.

"She's a truthful old dame!" he cried. "She's a kind old woman!"

"Dear me," said Mr. Straw, looking round. "That's your little goblin, isn't it? Well, it's nice of you to let me have the fresh cake, Mrs. Biscuit, when you've got one that is not quite so fresh. I'm much obliged to you. Perhaps you'll be good enough to come to my wife's birthday party this afternoon?"

"I'd be very pleased to," said Mrs. Biscuit, thankful that she hadn't given him the stale cake— for how dreadful it would have been to go to a birthday party and see everyone eating a stale cake she had sold as fresh!

Well, that was the last time Mrs. Biscuit ever thought of telling a story or being mean. She felt so nice when she had told the truth or been kind to someone that she soon found she simply couldn't tell a story or be unkind any more. And in a short time people liked her so much that they always bought their cakes and pies from her, and she became rich enough to buy a little cottage and go there to live.

She took the iced cake with her, with the little sugar house on top. She put it on a table in the front window to remind her of the days when she had kept a cake-shop—and would you believe it?—that Very-Little-Goblin is still there, shaking his carpet every day and opening his windows to let in the sunshine!

That shows she is still a truthful, kind old dame, and if you ever pass her cottage and see the iced cake in the window, with the little sugar house on top, don't be afraid of knocking at her door and asking if you may see the Very-Little-Goblin. Mrs. Biscuit will be delighted to show you round.

Midnight Tea-party

I PEEPED one night in the playroom,
   And I was surprised to see
The golliwog and the teddy
   Having their friends to tea!

The clockwork mouse and old Jumbo,
   The sailor doll and the clown,
And all the dolls from the doll's-house
   At the table were sitting down.

Golly had borrowed my tea-set,
   And Teddy was cutting a cake,
There were jellies a-shake in the dishes,
   And crackers for each one to take.

You think I was dreaming? I wasn't!
Today I found crumbs on the mat,
And jelly in one of the dishes,
   And the golliwog's blue paper hat!